HAPPINESS UNDER THE INDIAN TREES

the *Life-Story* of

CATHERINE CATTELL

by

Betty M. Hockett

GEORGE FOX PRESS

600 EAST THIRD STREET • NEWBERG, OREGON 97132

To
Edgar and Helen,
who mean so much to their daughter

HAPPINESS UNDER THE INDIAN TREES

The LIFE-STORY of Catherine Cattell

© 1986 George Fox Press
Library of Congress Catalog Card Number: 86-81349
ISBN: 0-943701-12-0

Second printing—November 1991

Cover by Lois A. Nelson
Illustrations by Phyllis M. Cammack

Litho in U.S.A. by The Barclay Press, Newberg, Oregon

CONTENTS

The Life-Story from Missions Series

FROM HERE TO THERE AND BACK AGAIN
*the life-story of Dr. Charles DeVol,
missionary to China and Taiwan.*

WHAT WILL TOMORROW BRING?
*the life-story of Ralph and Esther Choate,
missionaries to Burundi, Africa.*

DOWN A WINDING ROAD
*the life-story of Roscoe and Tina Knight,
missionaries to Bolivia, Peru, and Mexico City.*

HAPPINESS UNDER THE INDIAN TREES
*the life-story of Catherine Cattell,
missionary to India and Taiwan.*

CATCHING THEIR TALK IN A BOX
*the life-story of Joy Ridderhof,
founder of Gospel Recordings.*

MUD ON THEIR WHEELS
*the life-story of Vern and Lois Ellis,
missionaries to the Navajo Indians.*

WHISTLING BOMBS AND BUMPY TRAINS
*the life-story of Anna Nixon,
missionary to India.*

KEEPING THEM ALL IN STITCHES
*the life-story of Geraldine Custer,
missionary to Burundi, Africa.*

NO TIME OUT
*the life-story of George and Dorothy Thomas,
missionaries to Burundi and Rwanda, Africa,
and the Navajo Indians.*

*All by Betty Hockett, writer of Christian education
curriculum and stories for children.*

Chapter 1

THE MISSING SNAKE

Catherine DeVol thought it was rather fun to line up once a week with everyone else and wait for her turn to peek at the big black snake coiled inside the odd-shaped box. She considered it to be quite another matter the day they discovered the snake was missing.

Everyone at the Kuling School for Missionary Children had learned it was important to be orderly and quiet, no matter what! So, no one screamed or got all panicky, at least not noticeably so. However, Catherine *wished* she could scream. She certainly *felt* panicky. All she dared do was shiver anxiously and stand in line like everyone else was doing.

"Where can it be?" she wondered, feeling like she might explode any minute with this sudden fright that had ruined their normal routine.

"Children, back to your bedrooms, please!" said Mr. Lindsay, the school principal, whose snake it was. Everyone obeyed because that, too, was what they did at Kuling School.

"What if he's right here?" Catherine whispered to her best friend as they dropped onto their beds. She tucked her feet up under her and sat nervously waiting. "I don't know if this can be counted as a time to talk or not," she thought. She had discovered the hard way that at this school it was permissible to talk only at prescribed times. If anyone disobeyed, punishment was certain.

In all of her six years, Catherine had not come across anything as scary as not knowing where that big black snake was at that moment!

After a few minutes the teachers announced that the schedule would go on as usual. "I wish Mr. Lindsay would keep his monstrous snake somewhere else after this," Catherine thought on the way back to the classroom. "I don't care if I never get to peek again."

Before the day was over, Mr. Lindsay's worried frown was gone. "You don't have to be afraid any more," he announced cheerfully. "I found the snake. He was under the stairs."

Everyone smiled. Catherine felt much relieved. And that was the end of weekly peeks at the big black snake.

*　　*　　*

She mostly liked it at the China Inland Mission school located in the tidy little mountain village called Kuling there in central China. Climbing the

2

3,000 stone steps that led almost straight up was the only way to get to this village that was perched among the trees and rocks. It was there that missionaries went for a summer rest and where their children stayed on for school.

Catherine enjoyed having friends her own age. It was fun to play out under the trees and climb the mountains with the other missionary children who came from all over the world. In the town of Luho, China, where Catherine was born, she had been the only girl her age in the mission families. So she especially liked the girls at school, giggling and whispering secrets with them—all at the proper time, of course, when talking was allowed.

Her whole world for the first six years had been made up of a few Americans and many Chinese. "I feel like two people," she sometimes said. "Half of me is Chinese and half is American." When she was with the Chinese, she sat, ate, talked, and acted like they did. She was pure American when she was at home with her family. Catherine felt American at the Kuling school, too. It helped to have Charles,* her dear older brother, there with her. Of course, she missed little brother Ezra, who stayed at home with mother and father, Dr. Isabella and Dr. George DeVol. They were Friends missionaries who worked at Peace Hospital across from their home in Luho, down on the

---

* Read Charles' life-story in *From Here to There and Back Again*, also by Betty M. Hockett.

plains. She missed them, too, but had learned to be brave, even when she felt homesick. She was always glad when a message came that said, "Time to come home for a visit."

One day Catherine and Charles received a different message. It said, "Our family will be going to America on furlough soon." This would be Catherine's first trip to that faraway country.

"There isn't anyone who can go to Luho with you," Mr. Lindsay explained on the day the children were to leave Kuling. "But we can trust the chair coolies to take care of you." He tied the two DeVols securely into the sedan chair. The coolies lifted the load to their shoulders.

They had gone only a little way when a swift wind appeared, bringing with it a fierce rain. The coolies stopped right where they were and plunked the chair down on the ground. Then they hurried off to shelter!

Catherine and her brother soon were dripping wet. They wiggled and squirmed. "Mr. Lindsay tied us in too tight!" Catherine complained.

"He didn't want us to fall out," Charles replied, wiping the river that ran off the end of his nose.

Their fingers fumbled with the knots, pulling and tugging at the stubborn ropes. At last they gave way. The two of them climbed out and marched straight into the nearby teahouse.

Inside, the coolies were enjoying their cups of hot tea. "You must take us back to our school!" Charles said indignantly.

4

Catherine stood as tall as she could. She mimicked Charles' voice. "We can't go on like this. We're too wet!"

The coolies looked out over their teacups at the bedraggled children. "Well," one of them said reluctantly, "we will take you back to the school."

Before noon Catherine and Charles were back where they had started. Mrs. Lindsay met them at the door.

"Our other clothes have already gone down the mountain," the children said dismally.

The principal's wife gathered them into her arms, dripping clothes and all. "Never mind!" she said kindly. "We'll just borrow something for you to wear until these soaked clothes are dry."

*   *   *

Soon after the children arrived home at Luho, Dr. Isabella said, "You must have new clothes for our trip to the United States. But what shall we do? I can't sew at all!" She looked over the pile of used clothes donated by people in America. "I shall have to ask two of the other missionary ladies to help us."

These two, with the help of the Chinese tailor, created the things the three DeVol children needed. All but one thing, that is. "Catherine must have a hat!" Dr. George insisted.

They looked through the pile of hand-me-down clothes once more. "Here's one," someone said, holding up a hat that was obviously designed for a woman much older than Catherine.

Oh, well, we can fix it into a proper hat for Catherine," the ladies said. Needles, thread, and scissors soon changed the size and style of the hat. The artificial flowers and fruit the ladies arranged among bows and ribbons pleased Catherine.

"It's the most beautiful thing I've ever seen!" she exclaimed. Then the DeVols boarded a launch for the first part of their journey. "Goodbye!" they shouted. Their Chinese friends on the shore waved vigorously and sang, "God be with you." A brilliant shower of firecrackers unfurled like an umbrella over the whole scene.

Catherine held tightly to her hat with both hands. "You really ought to be waving back at everyone," her father said. "Here, take my handkerchief and wave it."

She took the hanky and waved it in the acceptable fashion. At that moment, a breeze blew along the water, sweeping Catherine's hat up and away.

Plop! Splash!

"My hat! My beautiful hat!" she cried. "It's in the river!"

"Oh, my!" exclaimed Dr. George. Everyone fluttered about, trying to think if there was any possible way to rescue the floating beauty.

Catherine was always able to see something funny in every situation. There was not anything funny about this, though. She felt as badly as the day when her only doll had fallen off and smashed

6

her head while on a donkey ride. She was almost sick as she watched the artificial flowers and fruit bobbing along with the wind and current.

"Oh, my!" Dr. Devol said again. "I am so sorry, Catherine. However, you *must* have a hat. The sun is entirely too hot for you to go without one." From then on he insisted she wear his white pith helmet.

And so, Catherine arrived in America for the first time, dutifully wearing father's hat, which was much too large. As soon as possible, mother and father bought Catherine a new hat all her own. It was exactly her size and style.

*   *   *

Sometime after the DeVols returned to China, the parents announced, "Catherine and Charles, we've made arrangements for you to go to school in Nanking. You'll live with the missionary ladies at the Quakerage and attend Hillcrest School."

"Nanking's only 25 miles from Luho," said Dr. Isabella with a smile. "You'll be able to get home more often."

Catherine had liked the school at Kuling but there would be some things she could do without. "No more sitting for an hour with my hands over my eyes if I talk too much," she thought. "And I hope no more lining up two times a week to have our knees inspected to see if there are holes in our long black stockings. Maybe at the new school we won't have to open our mouths so teachers can look down our throats and ask about everyone's health." She wrinkled up her nose at the thought of the doses of medicine poured down the open mouths each time.

And so, Catherine and Charles settled into life at the Quakerage with the four missionary ladies they called aunties. Charles' room was downstairs. The aunties occupied the four upstairs bedrooms. Catherine's room was upstairs, too . . . up the back stairs to the top landing, down a long hall and through a door that was always locked at night. When she heard the click of the lock, Catherine felt completely isolated from the rest of the house.

At night she dreaded going to her room. Charles always went with her. He stayed long enough to look around the room carefully, checking to make sure everything was all right. When he was sure, he would say, "Good night, Catherine," then head back down to his own room.

Catherine read Scripture every night. Nearly always she happened to turn to John 14:27: "Let not your heart be troubled, neither let it be afraid." Next, she repeated the two Bible verses Mother had helped her learn. "What time I am afraid, I will trust in thee," and "I will trust and not be afraid."

Every night she also said the prayer Dr. George had rhymed for his children.

> Our Father in heaven,
> We thank Thee tonight
> For food and for clothing
> For health and for sight.

Whatever of evil
This day I have done
Forgive me, dear Father,
Through Jesus, Thy Son.
And help me to live
Well pleasing to Thee
Now and forever
Thy dear child to be.
Bless Father and Mother
And all dear to me
The sick and the hungry
And all dear to Thee.

Sometimes, even after all of that, she cried softly into her pillow as she thought about home.

Living with the four dignified aunties was a blessing to Catherine. They were proper in every way. By nature they were stern but every now and then surprised Catherine by breaking into a round of giggles.

Most of all she loved the days when she received a letter from home. Father's letters always told how much he and Mother missed Catherine and Charles. He included a bit about Ezra and what he was doing there at home. Sometimes the letters had words of advice. "Catherine, you should spend more time practicing your writing. I know you could do better if you try." Or, "In order to be really happy, Catherine, you must do something every day to make someone else happy."

Catherine always tried harder. "I do want to please Father," she thought.

*   *   *

One Christmas at the Quakerage, a young missionary lady wanted to do something special. "I'm going to read the famous tale about Scrooge," she said, and proceeded to read the story in a way that completely captivated Catherine. The ghosts who came into Scrooge's dream made the story terribly exciting.

When the story was over it was time to go upstairs to bed. The ghosts of the story suddenly seemed quite real. Catherine walked up the stairs cautiously. Charles spent extra time looking around her room.

That night Catherine read more Scripture than usual. Then she did her best to go to sleep. Every time she closed her eyes, though, she could see the ghosts, one by one. She snuggled deeper into the blankets.

Suddenly she sat straight up. "I hear something! Something's coming up the stairs!" She began to tremble. The longer she sat listening, the more sure she was that she heard at least one of Scrooge's ghosts slowly walking closer and closer.

"Somebody'll lock the hall door for the night any time now and then I'll be alone with Scrooge's ghost until morning!" She was more frightened and lonely than she had ever been.

Chapter 2

"WHAT AM I TO DO?"

All at once Catherine scurried out of bed. She flew down the hall and into the room of one of the aunties.

"Catherine! What's wrong?"

"I think I heard Scrooge's ghost and I'm scared!" Catherine stood trembling in her long white nightgown.

"Dear me! Of course you are! Here, come sit in front of the fire with me." She took hold of Catherine's cold hand. "Now, let's count your blessings," she suggested.

Catherine shivered again. "A good father. A good mother. Food...school...church." She looked up at the auntie and smiled. "And kind aunties who let us live at the Quakerage."

They talked some more and Auntie prayed with Catherine before sending her back to bed. This time, the little girl remembered that God was with her. She did not find any sign of ghosts and soon she was sound asleep.

*   *   *

While they were at school in Nanking, Catherine and Charles heard about the serious illness of their father. They went home to Luho right away. One Sunday Catherine was sitting in front of the fire with another missionary, Auntie Holme. "There are many children, Catherine, whose fathers died in the war. Now they have to be brave so they can help their mothers during this sad time," Auntie explained.

As they were talking, Myrtle Williams, another missionary, came in. "Catherine," she said softly, "Your father is safe in Heaven."

Catherine thought a minute, realizing what that meant. "Ezra and Charles and I will have to be brave, won't we! Just like all those whose fathers died in the war, so we can help Mother."

A few months after Dr. George's death, Dr. Isabella became ill. It was not long until she and the children returned to America. Some friends in Ohio, Elbert and Martha Benedict, said, "Please make our home, Sunnyslope, *your* home."

Catherine was 13 years old by the time the DeVols arrived at the Benedict's large, comfortable farm home. She had to learn how to live a whole new kind of life away from China. She helped clean the 12-room house every Saturday. After meals there were piles of dirty dishes to wash in

12

the oversized stone sink. Stacked alongside were huge kettles, black with soot from the wood fire. They also needed a thorough scrubbing.

"I'm busy every minute of the day," she said to her mother. She did not want to complain. After all, Uncle Elbert and Aunt Martha, as everyone called them, were generous to offer their home to the DeVols.

The back porch was a favorite spot where Catherine often went at the end of the day. Here she could lean against the post and watch the sun slide gently down behind the patch of trees. It was a good place and a good time to think and pray about important questions. "What will happen to us? Will things ever be completely right again?" Long before, she had decided to be a missionary doctor in China. These days she could not help but wonder, "When will that be?"

She had no reason, then, to even consider that her life might take an entirely different course.

* * *

Dr. Isabella began to feel better. The family dared to dream of returning to China again. Then she became worse. In a short while she died. "Now I have no father or mother," Catherine thought sadly. However, God spoke to her and said, "I am your Father." She felt wonderfully comforted as God seemed closer to her than ever before.

Catherine and Charles had promised their mother that they would be missionaries to China.

13

"The time for us to go will come later," they told others. In the meantime, the three DeVols would be family for the Benedicts. Sunnyslope would be their home.

Aunt Martha helped Catherine learn many things. She showed her what real hospitality meant. The older lady's brand of hospitality was not something to do to show off a new rug or a special pie. It was given as a service for the Lord. Sunnyslope was often crowded with guests who were farm workers, evangelists, sick people, or missionaries on furlough. Catherine learned what it meant to "do for others." She endured the endless round of hard work. She did not know that all of these things she was learning would be put to good use someday when she had a home of her own.

Catherine had been a Christian for a long time. She was careful to obey God as best she knew. She and Charles were asked to speak at many meetings. "We want to hear about your experiences in China," people said. One evening Catherine attended a church meeting. Others were there from all around the area. At the close of the service the leader asked, "Will Catherine DeVol please dismiss us with prayer?"

And so, while 14-year-old Catherine prayed, another 14-year-old named Everett Cattell listened. He had met Catherine at other times, but this evening he really took notice of her. "I'm impressed," he told himself. "Imagine! Catherine praying in front of this whole crowd. Someday I'm going to marry her!"

Catherine and Everett met at summer conference for the next few years. They both worked to earn their way by serving in the dining room. One summer Everett said, "Catherine, if we could work together this week, we'd have the fastest and the most organized table going. Then all the bigwigs will want to come to our table. We'll show them how fast we can be so they'll get to their board meetings on time."

"That sounds like fun," said Catherine. Teamed together, they proved to be speedy and efficient. Conference attenders passed the word around. "If you want to get your meal in a hurry, sit at the table where Everett Cattell and Catherine DeVol are serving."

Catherine was busy with the work at Sunnyslope and travel to many meetings. Even so, she finished four years of high school classes in just three years. Next, she enrolled in Marion College, located in Marion, Indiana, where Charles also attended. Everett Cattell was a student there, too. Catherine began studying to be a doctor. She enjoyed college life, and her friends and teachers loved her. She and Everett were good friends. They spent time together. Sometimes Everett reminded her, "I want to marry you, Catherine."

Her answer was always the same. "I cannot marry you. I'm going to be a medical doctor in China and God has not called you to be a missionary." She knew, though, that Everett would make a perfect husband for her in every other way.

Just before graduation time, Catherine began to have troubles. First, her eyesight failed. She had always suffered some eye problems, but never this bad. The difficult classes at college had required lots of reading and a great amount of time spent in looking through microscopes.

"You must give your eyes complete rest," the doctor advised.

"Oh, my!" she thought. "If I can't look through microscopes how can I be a doctor? Everett wants to marry me and I want to marry him but he's not called to be a missionary. What am I to do?"

Catherine was confused. "I'll talk to Charles' mother-in-law," she decided. "Mrs. Van Matre will be a good person to help me."

She told her all about what was happening. "What am I to do?" she cried.

"Well, Catherine," said Mrs. Van Matre ever so gently. "Have you *really* been called to be a missionary to China?"

"Oh, of course!" Catherine replied quickly. "I've always planned to be a medical doctor in China."

"But I mean *really* called? Did *God* ever tell you to go to China?"

Catherine shook her head. "No, but I promised my mother I'd go."

"Do you think she would want you to go if God didn't tell you to go?"

Catherine and a friend, both wearing saris.

"No! But what am I to do?"

Mrs. Van Matre had a ready answer. "Start by saying, 'Lord, what do *You* want me to do?'"

Catherine thought of all the people who had sent money so she could study to be a doctor in China. "What will I say to them?" She remembered her friends on the mission board. "What will they think?" She felt like a thick black cloud had come down and wrapped itself tightly around her.

Catherine and Mrs. Van Matre got down on their knees beside the love seat. Catherine began to pray. "All right, Lord, I give myself completely to You. Maybe I don't really have a call to China after all. I'm just an American girl who doesn't know what to do next. And I don't like that feeling, Lord!"

This was the hardest thing Catherine had ever done. She cried and prayed for several hours. At 1:30 in the morning she told God, "I'm willing to do whatever *You* want me to do. I'm willing to stay right here in America. What You want will be fine with me." At last Catherine had peace.

Nevertheless, in the weeks to come she was not completely happy. Her eyesight continued to be poor. Others had to read the class assignments to her. By then she knew for sure she could not be a doctor. Charles and his wife, Leora, had already left for their first term of missionary service to China. She felt miserable and lonely.

When she told Everett the whole story, he was understanding and kind. "Then what's wrong with making plans for you and me to be married this summer?" he asked hopefully.

Catherine smiled in spite of tears. "Nothing, I guess! After all, I'm just an ordinary American girl now!"

And so they began to make plans for their marriage. This was the first step in serving God together in interesting places and through unforeseen circumstances.

Chapter 3

TEN NEW DRESSES

"You must have a respectable amount of clothes for your wedding trousseau, Catherine," encouraged her friends. "Ten dresses would surely be suitable."

"Ten dresses!" Catherine exclaimed in delighted astonishment. In all the years before she had never owned more than one or two dresses at a time. "That could include the white Chinese silk brocade Auntie Holme gave me," she added.

After the dresses were all made Catherine carefully packed nine of them, leaving the white brocade at Sunnyslope. It was exciting to have this many new dresses as she went to visit Everett and his family. Later she repacked the new dresses and set off to visit a friend in another Ohio town.

It was on this part of her journey that the suitcase loaded with her beautiful trousseau disappeared.

Catherine was heartbroken. She, along with others, organized a search. They advertised for the missing suitcase. They offered a reward to anyone who could find it. Days went by with no news.

She never saw her nine lovely new dresses again.

Ladies from the Missionary Society helped out by making another new dress. A friend made one more. This was her entire wedding trousseau, along with the white Chinese silk brocade.

Soon after their wedding Catherine and Everett drove to their new home, the parsonage of the Frist Friends Church in Columbus, Ohio. They wore old clothes and were well-equipped with brooms, mops, and buckets.

"We'll make everything spic and span before the truck gets here with our things," Catherine said enthusiastically.

All day long they scrubbed and polished. The time came for midweek prayer meeting that evening but the truck had not arrived. Catherine looked down at her blue cotton dress. It was spotted with washing powder and mop water. Her long brown stockings were stained at the knees from kneeling to scrub the splintery wood floor. The black, everyday shoes did not look good, either.

"I can't possibly go to prayer meeting looking like this," she moaned.

"The people are expecting us, though," Everett reminded. "They've been announcing that the new pastor and his wife will be there."

"Well, I do have the white brocade dress out in the car. But it isn't suitable to wear to prayer

Everett under the Indian trees.

meeting." She looked at herself again and sighed. "Well, I guess the only thing to do is to put it on anyway. It won't cover up the brown stockings and scruffy shoes but it's the best I can do."

Catherine was horribly embarrassed as they entered the church where the members would have their first glimpse of the newlyweds. Still, she suddenly saw the funny side of the situation. "O Everett," she giggled. "What a strange sight we are!"

* * *

The Cattells stayed at Columbus for three years. Then they moved to Springfield, Ohio, to a newly organized congregation, where they had a baby

21

boy named David. After that they went to live in Cleveland, Ohio, where Everett was the pastor at the First Friends church.

They invited Ezra DeVol to live with them while he attended medical school. Their daughter Barbara was born while they lived there.

"Everett, I think I could live happily here in Cleveland forever."

Everett agreed. "I think I could, too."

Not long after that, things began to change rapidly.

* * *

Catherine and Everett and their children gathered together with others from the church for a New Year's Eve service. They ate together, sang, and saw a slide show before it was time for prayer.

"I want to give you a special prayer request," said Everett. "We are needing new missionaries for our Friends mission in India. We may have to close the work entirely unless someone else will go. The mission board is calling for a couple to go and help with the work there."

"India is out of the question for us," Catherine thought. "If God wants us to be missionaries it would certainly be to China, not India." She knew she would never want to be a missionary to India, anyway. "I've always heard the mission there is difficult."

During the next few weeks Catherine could not forget the request for a couple to go to India. She prayed that someone would answer this call.

Catherine and Everett with villagers.

Then God said, "Catherine, why are you praying for someone to go where you are not willing to go yourself?" She was startled.

"I wish Everett wouldn't mention this in public again," she thought. She was beginning to feel uncomfortable about the matter.

Catherine soon realized Everett was thinking seriously about India. She felt more uneasy than ever. Finally she asked herself, "Does God want *us* to volunteer?" She prayed hard, just as hard as the time she had given up the idea of going to China.

Sometime later Everett said, "I've been thinking a lot about India."

"I have, too," Catherine confessed.

Everett was surprised. "I didn't suppose you would want to consider India."

"I don't," she replied truthfully. "I've been doing it, anyway."

"Do you suppose God wants us to say we'll go?"

From then on they could think of nothing else. "Let's apply to the mission board," Everett finally suggested. "No one else has, and I know that plans are underway to close the mission entirely there in India."

They prayed more and felt certain the Lord was calling them to India. Now was the time to talk it over with someone on the mission board. They got in their car and started down the road.

"Why do we think we could succeed in India?" asked Catherine. "India's a hard place to serve God."

"I've been thinking the same thing," said Everett. "It seems rather presumptuous to offer ourselves for India."

"Let's go back home!" Catherine suggested. "Nobody knows we've been thinking about this, anyway. And if God wants us to go to India, *He* can tell the mission board." With that, their minds were made up. Everett turned the car back toward home. That evening Catherine attended a graduation ceremony at the high school. When she returned, Everett said, "It's all settled, Catherine! We're going to India!"

She stared at Everett. "What...when...!" She could not wait to hear Everett's explanation.

Chapter 4

THE WISH

"I guess you're surprised," said Everett with a twinkle in his eyes.

Catherine nodded. "I should say I am!"

"While you were gone, one of the mission board members called on the phone. Imagine how I felt when he asked, 'Would you and Catherine consider going to India as our missionaries? If you can go, we won't have to shut down the mission work there.'"

Everett took a deep breath and went right on. "When I did not hesitate about saying 'yes,' he said, 'But what will Catherine think?' I told him you were ready to go."

Catherine put her arms around Everett and looked him straight in the eye. "Now we know for sure it's God's will that we go to India."

Right then and there they started getting things organized. In a few days they told their family and friends. Not everyone understood.

"Your children will surely die over there," some said gloomily.

"I don't fear India," Catherine replied. "I learned to love China, not fear it, and India is also the Orient."

*   *   *

The Cattells' first glimpse of India came from the ship as it steamed into the Port of Bombay. Little fishing boats dipped up and down on the harbor waves. Palm trees stood like guards along the shore. Catherine and Everett saw the dark-skinned faces of the Indian coolies waiting to help the passengers as they left the ship.

Catherine looked at the people and smelled the air. In the midst of the strange sounds she felt peaceful. "I'm happy to be here," she thought.

At the end of a long train ride the Cattells arrived in Nowgong. There they were to share the mission bungalow with Miss Esther Baird, another Friends missionary.

Nowgong was located in central India in an area called Bundelkhand. "It's funny, Everett," Catherine said one day, "I didn't expect the grass to be green and the sky to be this blue. And all these trees. Aren't they wonderful? The great spreading banyon trees with branches that touch the ground, and the large peepul trees! What would we do without them?"

"We'd get too hot," Everett replied. "I'm so glad that a long time ago a ruler ordered his workers to plant trees along the roads so travelers could go on in shade."

There were trees in their yard, out in the villages, in the jungles, and along the roads. There were so many different kinds of Indian trees, and Catherine was happy to be among them.

"From now on this is *my* land," Catherine said. "I already love it. I love the people, too."

Indian people were everywhere. Catherine saw them every day. "Such a variety of people," she thought, watching a group of coolies. These Indian workmen carried incredibly heavy loads that nearly hid the men themselves. Sometimes she saw the rajah and maharajahs riding by on horses or in rickshaws. The jewels these rulers wore sparkled in the bright sunlight.

Friends missionaries were the only ones bringing the Gospel to the enormous number of people living in Bundelkhand. The Indians there were from a variety of religions. Some were Hindus or Mohammedans. Others worshiped a god called Buddha. Also, there were different levels of society called *castes*: high caste, low caste, outcast, and several levels in between. It was all so different from anything Catherine and Everett had encountered before. "Every person in India is born into a certain caste," Catherine observed. "Everyone knows his place in life and keeps it."

"That's why some say that India is one of the hardest mission fields in the world," Everett added. "Everything Indians do or eat or wear has to be according to the rules of their caste. They can never get out of their caste, either. This way of life makes it hard for them to become Christians.

Just how hard was something Catherine and Everett would find out.

* * *

The four Cattells settled into the big bungalow with Miss Baird in the Christian community called a *compound*. Catherine and Everett learned all they could about the mission work, which included an orphanage, a hospital, and several schools. The missionaries were also in charge of the ministry of the church and work in the villages. Everett started out as superintendent of the mission. He had to remember to think about mission rules and Indian customs. He and Catherine began trying to speak a bit of Hindi, the language of the people in Bundelkhand.

Catherine laughed at their mistakes with the language. "The people seem pleased that we're trying, though," she said to Miss Baird, who assured her that their formal language study would be helpful.

Everett started arranging gospel meetings out in the countryside. He soon discovered some of the hard things about missionary work in India.

"Catherine, people in the village were interested but they couldn't come to our meeting," he reported after one trip. "They were forced to work for the maharajah instead."

Another time he came home saying, "This time the villagers couldn't come because a cow died. They were too busy claiming the meat."

Catherine nodded. She remembered that Indians never butchered a live cow. However, when a cow died, they were free to take the meat and eat it, even if it was rotten with disease.

While Everett was busy with his duties, Catherine took care of the household. She arranged for servants, not always knowing whether or not they were trustworthy. She nursed David and Barbara through malaria, measles, whooping cough, and infections from cuts. Indian servants cared for the children when she was occupied with studying or teaching Bible classes.

Five-year-old David soon was the darling of all who knew him. "He's made more friends for us than we could ever have made for ourselves," Catherine said.

Catherine's hospitality was generous. There were always cups of perfectly brewed hot tea for all who came to their home. All kinds of people became part of her life — English, Indian, American, rich, poor, Christian, Hindu, city folks, and village people. She had a natural ability to understand these interesting people.

She was especially concerned for the Indian women, no matter what their religion happened to be. The baggy pants and knee-length dresses that some wore intrigued her. She was interested in the headdresses called *burkahs* that entirely covered the face of the wearer. Catherine admired the expensive silk cloth that the wealthy women draped into graceful full-length garments called *saris*. Poor village women also wore saris, but their fabrics did not cost so much.

"I wish I could do something for these beautiful Indian women," she thought. The more she got acquainted with them, the more she realized how lonely many of them were. Some could not read or write, and most were superstitious and fearful.

Catherine looked for opportunities to visit the women. Sometimes she went to homes of women who belonged to a high caste. Mary Bai, an elderly woman, often went with her.

"We must find a way to introduce the Gospel to these women," Catherine said. The two sat with the Indian women in their courtyards, which were hidden behind high walls. They taught some of them how to knit. They also taught them to read. Mary Bai and Catherine always sang a Christian song, then spent time explaining what the words meant. One or the other of them told a Bible story each time, too.

Catherine continued to be interested in all Indian women, not just those of high caste. "I wish I could go out into the villages," she said to Everett. "I know the gospel message would make a difference in the lives of those women. They're so awfully poor with so little they can call their own. No one pays much attention to them."

"You're right," Everett said. "But you'll have opportunity to go sometime. When the children are old enough to go along."

"And when there will be others who can stay to oversee the orphanage and the work here while we're in the villages," Catherine added thoughtfully. "I'm eager for the time when I can sit out under the trees where the Indian women will gather to listen to me tell about God. In the meantime, though, I'll do what I can for the Christian women here at the compound." They were the only happy Indian women she had seen.

She started Bible classes for them. Her language teacher spent extra time helping her prepare the lessons with the correct Hindi words. Once a week she met with the women, studying the Bible and talking about their family responsibilities. They sewed for the orphan children and made things for the hospital. Little by little these women who had grown up in the mission orphanage became interested in others. "We should be telling more people about Jesus," they said.

Catherine was pleased. This was exactly what she had prayed would happen. She helped the women choose a lesson, then they all practiced it together. After memorizing Scripture verses, they were ready to go out and share what they had learned.

* * *

Catherine often watched Everett and the Indian evangelists load up for their journeys out into the villages. "How soon will I have the privilege of going along?" she wondered. "It seems such a long time before there will be opportunity for the women out there to hear the Gospel."

When the men returned, they sometimes brought this report: "There were several men interested in the Gospel. However, their wives threatened to leave them if they became Christians."

"We *must* get the Gospel out to the women," Catherine said firmly. She looked at David and Barbara. They were growing up. Soon they would be big enough to go along on the rigorous trips into the villages. "Someday I will be out there under the trees, teaching the women," Catherine said with renewed hope.

However, she had no idea about the frightening things that would happen in the meantime.

Chapter 5

THE NIGHTMARE

Catherine listened as the doctor said, "Everett, you need to have your appendix removed. It's a simple operation, you know."

They made arrangements for a ten-day leave. Catherine planned to go with Everett to the hospital, 80 miles away. The children would stay behind.

Just as the doctors were beginning the operation, Everett unexpectedly became extremely sick. "He's dying!" the nurses announced. They rushed around, assisting the doctors who were just barely able to save his life.

"This seems like a nightmare," thought Catherine. This nightmare lasted for the next three months.

Catherine lived in the home with the missionary doctors and nurses. Every night she heard them despair. "Surely Mr. Cattell will die tomorrow."

She spent most of her time alone in her room in the house or beside Everett's bed. No one had time to comfort her. She was lonely.

One night she realized there was a flurry of activity. "It's an emergency about Everett," she thought as a shiver of fear swept over her. Immediately Catherine fell to her knees.

"Oh, God," she prayed. "What can I do if I'm left here in India alone with two children? I need my husband!" The fear rolled across her like ocean waves, over and over.

"Trust Me, Catherine," God seemed to say. "Remember, I called you here to India."

"I know for sure You did call us, Lord. And even if Everett dies I'll know You called us. But please save his life because he's needed here for the work You called us to do."

All at once Catherine thought, "I mustn't tell God who He needs!" She went on praying. At last she was able to say, "Dear God, I give Everett into Your hands."

When she opened her eyes, she saw a Bible verse: "With long life will I satisfy him and show him my salvation." Suddenly she rose from her knees. She felt gloriously free.

"He's going to be all right. That verse is God's promise!"

The next day, Everett's condition was worse!

"I must read this verse to him even though he's unconscious," she thought, starting through the hot, dry yard on her way to the hospital.

The woman doctor came toward her. "I think I'm losing this case and if I do, I'll never practice medicine again," she said tearfully.

Catherine smiled and reassured her. "It's going to be all right. I have a verse."

"Hang onto that verse. That's the only hope we have!" the doctor replied.

"And there's something else I want to tell you," Catherine said. "A few minutes ago a peddler came along with two wicker chairs for sale. I bought both chairs. They're on the verandah now. You see, some day Everett will sit in one of them and I'll sit beside him in the other. That's a promise. I'm going to call them our *faith chairs.*"

All through this nightmare people in many parts of India were praying for Everett. People from many denominations and beliefs were asking God to perform a miracle and make him well. In fact, people in different places around the world were praying for him.

Everyone was pleased when the day came that they could see Everett showing definite signs of getting well. At last the nightmare was over!

* * *

Now Catherine could think again about going out into the villages to take the Gospel to the women. The day finally came when it was all right for her to do what she had wanted to do for so long.

Catherine, Barbara, and the wife of an Indian evangelist loaded themselves and their traveling gear onto the public lorry. The back of the truck bulged with their cots, pails, lanterns, boxes of food, bedding, folding chairs, and sacks of charcoal fuel. The lorry rattled off down the bumpy, dusty road toward the village called Launri, 40 miles away.

Catherine watched eagerly for the first sight of the village where Everett, David, and the Indian evangelist were already at work. All at once, there it was, under the big cluster of mango trees.

"What a lovely place!" she thought, feeling a new rush of excitement.

She was happy out under the trees. The peepul trees, mohwa and silk-cotton trees made great blotches of protection from the searing Indian sun. The red springtime blossoms on the "flame of the forest" trees created brilliant spots of color. David helped brush away the animal dirt and make a place to sit under the trees. As Catherine played her harmonium, the loud music drew the women's attention.

She knew there was so much she had to learn. "I don't know how to make my messages fit the situations of these women," she thought, as the Indian women gathered, chattering freely in Bundelkhandi.

"At least I'm here," she said to Everett that evening. "I will sit where they sit. I will learn about these women and how they think. I will find out what they want and need. I want to help them understand the message of God's love."

This first camping trip out in the Indian villages lasted for a month. It was just the beginning of much happiness, serving the Lord out under the Indian trees.

*   *   *

The Cattells moved to Chhatarpur, a few miles away from the mission compound at Nowgong. Working with the Indian women became Catherine's special assignment. She worked with women of the church, those sick in the hospital, and village women. She traveled out to the villages by oxcart, jeep, lorry, or bicycle, sometimes staying ten days at a time. She learned how to live simply like the Indian women. "I want them to think about the Bible lesson, not about how different I look," she explained, and practiced wearing the lovely Indian dress. Rather than having a plentiful supply, she "made do" with only two saris. "Just like the poor Indian village women," she said.

Each time she was out under the trees she sat by the village well, or squatted beside the women as they tended their cooking fires. She continually found new ways of showing love and compassion. Catherine was happy out there.

"I need to know something about simple medical treatments," she told Everett, "Many of these people never see a real doctor." She learned how to treat sores and discovered which pills were appropriate for certain illnesses.

One day in a meeting under the trees alongside the village well, a small girl took up the offering. When she returned the money to Catherine she smiled in a shy way. "Someday I will be a Christian," she said. "And when I am grown up and married, my whole family will be Christians, too."

"I hope she can keep that promise," Catherine thought. "It's so hard for these women to become Christians."

Out under the trees Catherine taught other things to the women besides Bible lessons. She helped them know how to improve their home life. She gave them instructions in different kinds of handwork.

In between visits to the villages Catherine did writing. She prepared a booklet for the young people. She held classes for the women in town.

Meantime, Everett was busy also. It seemed that for both of them there was always more to do than there was time. They were encouraged that at last some of the Indian workers and their families had moved out to the villages, away from the compound.

"These families are lonely," Everett said. "I think we should go out and spend a few days in each home."

"Yes," Catherine agreed. "We could bring comfort and cheer to them."

Early one hot and muggy August morning, Catherine and Everett loaded their bicycles with mosquito netting, a change of clothes, food and water, the medicine kit, bedding, and their raincoats. They started out to a town 15 miles away, on the other side of the thorn bush jungle. The narrow path was hard to follow. In one place they nearly lost it completely. By noon the sun was unbearably hot.

"We must stop here under this big banyon tree for lunch," Everett said.

Toward evening they arrived at the village on the edge of a lake. They were met by a pack of naked children who immediately tore off through the town shouting, "The white-skinned Sahib and Memsahib are here! They're on their way to stay all night at the Christians' house!"

The Cattells parked their bikes in front of the pastor's house. A crowd gathered immediately. Catherine heard one old woman say to their hostess, "I came to see if you need anything." Another one said, "I did, too!"

Catherine leaned over to Everett and whispered, "The real reason they came is that they want to see what's going on." Everyone was friendly. Soon, though, the villagers had enough looks and went on their way.

The missionaries and the Indian pastor and his wife were left by themselves. The wife was sitting in a corner of her kitchen making *chapatis*. The sight of this good whole wheat bread and also the fragrance of vegetables cooking with spices made Catherine feel hungry.

Just then the pastor handed her a brass cup of hot tea boiled together with sugar and goat's milk. "This tastes good," she said gratefully.

That night Catherine and Everett slept outside in the courtyard, listening to the snores of the oxen that slept in one of the rooms close by. Once again Catherine was happy for the privilege of experiencing what the Indians experienced every day.

"I'm glad you came to see us," said the Indian pastor the next morning. "Especially for the sake of my wife. She seldom sees another Christian woman."

Catherine sat with the pastor's wife in the small, hot room filled with smoke. They talked and prayed. When the visit was almost over, the Indian woman opened the lid of a tin box. She held up a piece of lovely handwork.

"I made this when I was young," she said. "I planned to keep it for use in my home. But where in this smoky room would I put it?" She handed the white cloth to Catherine. "Please take it. When you use it, think of me. It will make me happy. I hope you come to see me again."

The Cattells started back over the same difficult 15 miles toward home. "Our idea of visiting the pastors was a good one," said Catherine happily. She trudged along, thinking of so many things they still needed to do out under the Indian trees. Some of these things yet to be done would end up in happiness for them. Other things would not.

Chapter 6

A STRANGE BROWN CLOUD

"Now that it's spring again, it's time to think about organizing another jungle camp," said Everett.

Catherine remembered how successful the first one had been the year before.

"This time we'll go to a new location in a larger grove of trees," the missionaries decided. "And we'll build little palm-leaf huts as well as set up tents where people can stay."

Groups of Indians arrived and jungle camp number two got underway. Sunday evening, just as the evangelist began preaching, people on the edge of the crowd became distracted.

"Look at that strange brown cloud," they said, pointing nervously to the eastern sky.

Soon everyone noticed the unusual cloud. Within minutes the whole landscape looked eerie, as if it was painted with that strange brown color. A powerful wind struck the camp at the same time. The wind and a downpour of rain brought the meeting to an immediate halt.

"Rush to your huts or tents and do what you can to save your things. Everyone must take refuge," Everett shouted over the wind.

Catherine ran through the rain to rescue their evening meal that had been cooking under the trees. As she got there, the tent poles were wobbling dangerously. It was all she and their cook could do to keep the tent from collapsing.

The whole camp was in complete chaos. The lights were out, every tent was flapping crazily, huts had blown away, and everything was soaked.

The storm lasted 20 minutes. As the wind and rain calmed, Catherine heard the children crying. Voices of wives calling to their husbands carried plainly. "The whole countryside is flowing like a river," she thought. "All that preparation, and now everything's ruined!"

"No, Catherine, not unless you let it be," said God.

"Well, yes! That's right!" she decided. Soon she was laughing at how funny everything and everybody looked. "A good hot cup of tea will help revive us," she announced, and set about to help those around her.

The weather was beautiful for the rest of the week and the meetings continued. In spite of the bad beginning, jungle camp turned out well. "This will help us remember that circumstances don't shut off God's power and blessing," Catherine reminded the others.

*   *   *

A few days before one Easter, Catherine thought about a certain Indian family. "They're lonely and discouraged. We must go to spend Easter with this Christian worker and his family who live way out there at Isanagar," she said.

She knew this meant traveling through long stretches of teakwood trees and thornbush jungle as well as across dry river beds. Besides, it was the season when the hot winds would scorch them as they traveled. "But it's important for us to make Easter a time of happiness for these dear people," she said. "They've suffered so much this year. Their daughter died and their crops failed. Then, too, they're thoroughly discouraged because there are no other Christians in their village."

It was a rough trip, bouncing along in the ox tonga that was full of their luggage. By evening the travelers turned the corner at the top of a steep hill. Out before them was the village on the shore of a lovely lake. They easily located the Indian home and received a joyful welcome.

Catherine looked around at the cluttered rooms. "How can we help this discouraged family celebrate Easter?" she asked herself. There's nothing here to work with except this plain, crowded little house. And it's up to me to plan our celebration."

Catherine stayed awake far into the night. Even in the dark the black rafters overhead were unsightly. Pieces of rags drooped helter-skelter

43

over them. "There's no church room here," she thought. "Just this room that's overflowing with cart wheels and grain and beds. How can we clean it up to make it a worshipful place? I don't want to offend the family."

With only the nighttime sounds, Catherine prayed. Gradually she thought of what they could do.

The next morning she explained the plan. "There are 11 of us here. We'll divide into committees and everyone can help. That way there won't be so much work for our kind host and hostess."

Catherine looked at the two Indian women who had come along. "You are much better at helping with the cooking than I am, so you and our hostess can prepare the meals and do the regular housework. The rest of us will be the decorating committee."

Everyone nodded and smiled agreeably.

"Will it be all right if we take everything out of the room in front so we can make it into a churchroom?" Catherine asked, a bit cautiously.

"Oh, yes," said the host and hostess.

Right after everyone finished their tea and fried wheat cakes, the committees got busy. The men carried the cart wheels outside. They scooped up the grain and pulled the rags down from the rafters. Then they hung fresh palm branches to hide the ugly boards. Someone swept the mud floors and brushed the cobwebs from the walls. Everyone was pleased with how attractive the room looked.

That afternoon Catherine led the women to the lake to gather flowers. "These lotus blossoms will look lovely in with the palm branches," she said.

The pastor, his wife, and their guests were all up and dressed by four o'clock on Easter morning. They walked out by lantern light to the top of the hill at the edge of town. The first rays of light were coloring the sky. The delicate colors of the sunrise shone in the lake.

As far as Catherine could see, village lights twinkled all across the Bundelkhand landscape. "Jesus came to be the Light of the world," she thought. She and the others sang enthusiastically. The pastor read the Bible story about Jesus arising from the grave. Then they started back to the house, singing more songs along the way. Now and then they stopped and stretched their arms wide and shouted praises to God.

Later it was time for the morning service. Many of the villagers came, crowding into the small home. The ladies wore their best saris and the men were in dress-up suits. Someone spread a blanket on the floor where several of the worshipers could sit. The fragrance of the lotus flowers filled the room.

"It's beautiful in here," the people said. No home in Isanagar had ever looked this way before.

The next morning, the wife of the pastor said, "I dreaded Easter this year. We have had so many discouragements. I have been lonely since our little girl died, but the thought of Jesus being alive comforts me. This has turned out to be a happy time. Thank you for coming."

She handed a small bundle to each of the visitors. "I don't have much to give you, but here, take this little bit of rice. It's from our fields."

Her husband smiled and added, "I like the way you made our front room into a church-room. I feel like keeping it nice for church."

"Thank You, Lord," thought Catherine. "You did help us make this Easter turn out to be a special time."

*   *   *

Catherine and Everett had been in India over six years. Exciting things had happened but there were discouraging things, too. They both felt exhausted.

"We need a complete change," Catherine said. "I'm glad it's time for us to go back to the United States for a rest."

A few days after that Everett said, "There isn't anyone to take our place here, Catherine. And you know we can't leave without someone being here."

She looked straight at Everett without saying anything. Catherine was not sure she wanted to hear what he was going to say next.

Chapter 7

DISAPPOINTMENT

Everett continued the conversation. "Since World War II is still on it's difficult for us to get passage to go home, anyway. So, Catherine, the mission board suggested that we stay on in India for the duration of the war."

"What a disappointment!" Catherine thought. She longed to see her friends and family in Ohio. Knowing she and Everett and the children would not be going now made her feel sad and lonely.

Walking to the back of the house, she found Ramki Bai. The wife of the Indian evangelist was calmly sitting on the ground grinding her spices on a flat stone. Catherine sat on the corner of the rope bed beside Ramki Bai.

"I need a friend to talk to," she said quietly. Then she told the Indian woman about her disappointment and loneliness. "I want to go home so badly. I want to see my own people!"

Ramki Bai looked peaceful and content. Somehow, just seeing her made Catherine feel better.

47

All at once she thought, "Ramki Bai is part of my family. My wonderful dear Indian family! She and all of my Indian women are my people! Why do I need to go to the United States? Some of my people are right here!" From that moment on, she felt better.

*　　*　　*

Everett was often away in evangelistic work. One of the times he was gone, Catherine stayed longer than usual in the mountains near the boarding school where Barbara and David attended.

"I need to go back down on the plains to get to work," Catherine told God one day. "You know, though, there's not enough money. During the war we aren't receiving our money from the United States. What do You want me to do?"

"Sell what you have," God told her.

She gathered up some of the things she knew her family could do without. The electric iron, a few empty bottles and several cans—she sold them all but still there was not enough money. Catherine looked in the cupboard to see what else she could find.

She spied her blue dishes! "I don't want to sell them," she thought forlornly. I've only just bought them. It's the first time I've ever had such really nice dishes for entertaining."

She looked at the dishes a bit longer, then sighed. "I guess, though, God meant what He said." She put the lovely cups and saucers into a basket with a set of everyday dishes. The blue

48

plates went in, also. She hung the basket over one arm and set out through the rain.

Catherine walked along the path to the home of another missionary. "She does a lot of entertaining. I know she has dishes like these so perhaps she'll want more."

She told the story to the servant who answered her knock. "No!" he said quickly. "We don't need any more dishes."

Catherine's hope was gone. "What shall I do now?" She started to leave, but stopped when she heard the missionary call from inside, "Who's out there?"

"Catherine Cattell," replied the servant.

"What's she doing?"

"Trying to sell some dishes."

Catherine's missionary friend appeared at the open door. She looked into the basket. "Of course we want those dishes. We must have them!" She ushered Catherine inside. "Here, sit beside the fire," she insisted and handed out a delicious hot cup of tea. She paid for the purchase and prayed with Catherine before allowing her to go home.

Now Catherine had enough money to go down out of the mountains and get on with her duties. In a few weeks she received a ten-dollar bill from the same missionary. A note with it said, "Money is coming to us. I feel the Lord wants me to send this to you."

"Thank You, Lord," said Catherine. "This is just enough to pay my cook and buy the things we need this month."

The next month another ten dollars came. It was exactly the right amount for that month, too. Throughout the rest of the war the same thing happened every month. When the war emergency was over and the Cattells received their regular allotment from the mission board in the United States, the missionary in the mountains no longer sent the monthly gift.

"I'll never forget what she did for us," Catherine said thankfully. "She had no idea what we needed or for how long we needed it. We did not tell her. God did."

*   *   *

Finally, after nearly ten years in India, Catherine and Everett returned to the United States. They made their headquarters at Sunnyslope with Catherine's brother Ezra and his family. Her older brother Charles was there, too, with his family. It was a happy time for the three DeVols.

Important things happened that year. Mary Catherine Cattell was born. Catherine wrote a book called *Till Break of Day*, and Everett had two serious operations. In between everything else, they traveled on an intensive deputation tour.

At the end of the year they returned to India. "To continue the work God has called us to do," said Catherine. Their Indian friends were happy to get acquainted with the new little Cattell.

Catherine was good at creating a comfortable home for her family, regardless of where they lived. In a matter of minutes after arriving at a new location, she could place a few familiar things around and the family would feel at home. One year she covered old trunks with bright cloth, turning them into sofas. She had a special knack for arranging fresh flowers. "She's an amazing interior decorator," others said.

The special Sunnyslope hospitality was noticeable in the Cattell home. "Catherine's always ready for company," other missionaries said. "No matter who comes to her home, she never forgets to offer a good hot cup of tea and something to eat. Everyone seems to be welcome."

Catherine often said to her children, "Happiness comes by giving it away to someone else." She was generous, too. Once when Mary could not find her sweater, Catherine said, "I gave it to someone who needed it worse than you."

Throughout her busy days as a missionary, Catherine was never too occupied but that she had time to be supportive of her family. She prayed for them and longed to see their three children close to God themselves.

The years hurried past. Catherine wrote a book on Bundelkhandi grammar to help the new missionaries have an easier way of learning the difficult dialect. She also began the Women's Retreat, held once a year in a village or out under the jungle trees. The Indian Christian women of Bundelkhand came and found spiritual help each time. Catherine also led Bible studies for the nurses at the hospital. She was happy when Ezra and his wife, Frances, came with their children to be missionaries in Bundelkhand, too. Ezra was a medical doctor and Frances was a nurse.

David and Barbara went back to the United States to go to school. "Nothing here is like I remembered it," David wrote. His parents knew he was unhappy and having a hard time. This made them feel sad.

"Don't worry, I am able to take care of David," God said to Catherine and Everett. Later they rejoiced when David wrote, "I've given my life back to God. When I'm finished with school I want to return to India as a missionary."

Nobody knew then that something else would happen instead.

* * *

Catherine was happy each time she went out to the villages and sat in the shade under the trees with the Indian women. She loved the women and wished for better ways of presenting the Gospel to them. "Or better yet, if there were lessons they could use themselves to teach others," she thought.

Then Mary developed a severe back problem. "This comes because of the bad fall she had several years ago," the doctor explained. "She must stay in bed until it is healed."

Catherine teaching with a flannel board.

"I will gladly stay home and take care of Mary," said Catherine. She realized it would mean a long time away from her work. Everett was scheduled for more preaching trips during the next weeks.

"Perhaps this is the time you should do some writing," he suggested.

Catherine perked up at this idea. "I could write the lessons I've been wishing for."

She went to the dentist a few days after that. There she visited with a young woman from another mission.

"What are you doing these days?" the young woman asked.

"I'd like to write lessons for the village people but I need an artist to draw pictures to go along with them."

"I'm an artist."

"You are?" replied Catherine. "I'm surprised. I thought you were a nurse."

"I am, but I like being an artist better."

"Maybe you're the answer to my prayers," said Catherine. After they talked more, the young woman said, "I could help you take care of Mary and draw the pictures you need, too."

Right away she made the arrangements with her mission so she could live with the Cattells. Catherine worked on the lessons every day. She wrote ten lessons for people who were not Christians and ten more lessons for those who already had accepted Christ. Each lesson had the exact Scripture verses and the words the teacher should say.

The artist drew pictures for each lesson. She included clear directions about how to use the pictures. Catherine decided the book should be named, *That They May Know*. She thanked God for His help, and also prayed, "May this little book go places that I never will be able to go."

The Indian Christians were able to use the lessons as Catherine hoped. Eventually they were translated into several Indian dialects. After a time, Christian workers in the little country of Nepal used the book, also. Thousands of people

Catherine and Everett Cattell

understood the Gospel when they heard the lessons and saw the pictures.

*   *   *

One day when Everett was away, Catherine saw the
messenger boy approaching with the bag of mail.
"I have a feeling that something really important is
in that bag," she thought uneasily.

"Good foreign mail today, Memsahib," the boy
said cheerily.

Hesitating a moment, she reached for the bundle of mail. She did not know why she felt as she did. As soon as she saw what one of the letters said, she knew why. "We would like you to return to America so Everett can be the superintendent of Ohio Yearly Meeting of Friends."

"What a surprise!" Catherine mumbled to herself. "Will Everett consider this offer?" In the next breath she said out loud, "Oh, I hope not!"

Suddenly India had never looked so beautiful. In all the years they had been there she had never loved the Indian people as much as she did at that moment. Her desire to help them become Christians was greater than ever.

In a few days Everett arrived home and read the letter. He spent time thinking and praying about the matter. "Yes, I believe this is the time for us to leave India," he said.

"Then if this is our last year in India, it must be our best," Catherine answered.

They were busy working with the Indian churches and leading conferences for the Christian workers. God promised that He would be faithful to go with them wherever they went. His assurance was comforting. It was especially so when the government made new rules that prevented the missionaries from traveling about the country as much as usual.

The time came closer for them to leave India. There were surprises ahead for Catherine and Everett.

Chapter 8

AN UNEXPECTED MESSAGE

Catherine looked at the calendar. "Just a few more days and our 21 years in India will be over," she said, then packed the last box and took one more look around. "Come, Mary, we're ready to go now and stay with Uncle Ezra and Aunt Frances until we leave."

Catherine walked out of the house with a firm step, in spite of the sadness she had felt since the day trouble began for their Indian Christians.

"And to think it's our David's good friend who is one of those stirring up the commotion," she thought. "If only he had stayed true to the Lord. Sin brings such awful consequences!"

She had no idea, then, just how much trouble this young man would cause before the whole thing was over.

A few days later, Catherine and Everett met another young man who said, "Sahib, you are soon going to be arrested for ruining the reputation of your former preacher!"

Catherine gasped! The young man continued. "Two Indian church leaders will be arrested, too. It's dangerous for me to tell you this but I wanted to warn you. There are other charges against you, too. I know, of course, that none of the charges are true."

The young man stepped closer to Everett and lowered his voice. "Some of your friends have turned against you. Your true friends do not want to see you humiliated in this way. Please leave India right away!"

Catherine and Everett stood there in horrified silence. Finally Everett said, "I cannot leave my Indian friends to face these untruths alone."

The next day as Catherine and Everett were eating lunch with the DeVols, the police came. They arrested Everett and two Indians. "But you may stay here in this house until the trial," they said. "It would be too troublesome to arrange for your food if you went to the jail."

The Cattells learned that David's boyhood friend had agreed to say that Everett furnished guns to bands of robbers. He also told the troublemakers that Everett had paid people to become converts.

"What ugly lies!" said Catherine in disgust.

Everett was not feeling well and the extreme heat of the season made him feel worse. Some of the missionary women fell seriously ill with typhoid fever. Mary's health was fragile, too.

"O God, how I need Your hand to lead me and hold me!" Catherine prayed desperately.

As bad as things were just then, the worst was still to come.

The other missionaries and some of the Indian Christians met together, then said to Everett and Catherine, "All of this turmoil along with the heat will be too stressful for Mary. We urge you and Mary to go immediately to the city of Jhansi, Catherine."

"How can I leave Everett here alone?" Catherine thought. Then she knew that for Mary's sake she must do as the others suggested. She would trust Everett to the care of Ezra and Frances.

Many times each day there in Jhansi, Catherine reminded herself, "God is with me!" Even when she heard the date for Everett's trial, she said, "God is holding my hand!"

Then came August 8, the day of the trial. In the middle of the morning, a servant came running into the office where Catherine was working. "Memsahib, a car from your mission has just arrived. The people are calling for you."

Catherine hurried after the servant. She went into the long sitting room of the mission house. There before her was Everett. Ezra and Frances sat nearby. Frances was crying.

Everett gently took Catherine's hand. "Sit down," he urged. "We have sad news." He swallowed hard and slowly told his wife, "We've received word from the United States that David, his wife, Jane, and their baby girl have all been killed in a terrible car crash."

Catherine was stunned. She looked from one to the other. "How can this be?" she asked weakly. "Their baby—our granddaughter—we've never seen her. They were hoping to come to India next year and we were so happy about that!"

In the days that followed, Catherine heard God speak words of comfort and strength to her. She was glad that for the time being the court had excused Everett from his trial.

It was not only the Cattells who mourned David's death. The Indians, who had loved him did, too. Many of the Indian Christian women came to sit beside Catherine in her sorrow.

"You came to sit beside us when we sorrowed," they said.

Catherine sent a message to David's friend. "I want you to know that David has died. His wife and child, too."

Early the next morning this young man who had turned against the Cattells appeared at their door. Catherine saw that he looked troubled. "My husband is at your mercy, you know. Have you forgotten God?"

The young man sobbed. "No, I have not forgotten. Memsahib, someday I will do the work of David and me both. I will come back!"

Just as the trial was to begin once again, Frances DeVol became ill with typhoid fever. This time the missionaries and Indian Christians urged

Catherine to take Mary and leave India entirely. It was another difficult decision. "Yes," she agreed, "Mary and I will go to Taiwan right away. We can stay with Charles and Leora."

Even though she could hardly bear to leave Everett behind, Catherine took Mary's hand. Together they boarded the airplane for Taiwan. She remembered that God was the One holding *her* hand.

"Welcome to Taiwan!" exclaimed Charles as he and his wife engulfed Catherine and Mary in big hugs.

Catherine took one look at the missionaries and Chinese Christians gathered there. "Charles, please take me somewhere to rest. I'm not ready to meet lots of people."

"Oh, no," Charles replied pleasantly. "You are to be at one of our churches tonight and they'll want to hear a few words from you."

"But Charles! I haven't spoken Chinese since I was a child. And...."

"Never mind, Catherine. These are the plans." Charles hastened to outline the schedule of events.

For ten days Catherine visited churches on the little island of Taiwan. She felt comforted by the love and understanding of the Chinese Christians, who wept upon hearing of David's death. She made many new friends and was surprised to see some people she had known long ago in China.

One day they went to the dedication of a new church. Catherine sat in a place of honor on the platform. "This is where Everett should be sitting," she thought, once again feeling lonely.

As the audience sang a hymn, Catherine glanced out the open front door. A man with a yellow envelope in his hand was getting off his bicycle. Charles also saw the man. He rushed outside to receive the envelope.

Catherine's heart suddenly beat faster. "That envelope has news for me. Good news or bad, I don't know!" She waited tensely as her brother tore open the envelope and came back to the platform to make an announcement.

Barbara, Mary, and David Cattell

Chapter 9

A NEW LIFE

Charles made the announcement in a clear voice. "Everett and the two Indian men have been acquitted. Everett is on the way to Taiwan right now!"

Catherine sighed deeply. "Thank You, God, for answering our prayers and helping the court know he was not guilty!"

The dedication service immediately turned into a celebration. The Chinese rejoiced with Catherine just as heartily as they had sorrowed with her.

When Everett arrived, he told them everything that had happened. "Our Indian Christians prayed hard all during the trial. They kept telling me, 'The Lord will be with you.'"

Catherine squeezed his hand lovingly and listened as he continued. "The last morning, Ezra read Jeremiah 40:4 in our regular morning devotions. That verse says, 'And now, behold, I loose thee this day from the chains which were upon thine hand...whither it seemeth good and convenient for thee to go, thither go.' That was God's promise that I would be set free."

"But what about our young Indian friend?" Catherine inquired, feeling more relaxed than she had felt for a long time.

"He told the truth, Catherine. And the people who had accused me of doing wrong were thoroughly disgusted at how it all turned out."

*   *   *

Catherine, Everett, and Mary arrived in the United States on a Sunday. The next morning Everett stepped into his office as superintendent of Ohio Yearly Meeting of Friends. Mary enrolled in elementary school.

Catherine felt somewhat overwhelmed. She had lived more years in China and India than in the United States. She wanted their home to be a comfortable place where she could be hospitable. "I don't know how to entertain American style," she moaned. Quickly she decided, "I'll do it the way I know best."

Catherine arranged their basement into the likeness of an Indian home. She entertained there in Indian style. Guests sat on the floor and ate the Indian food with their fingers. They were delighted and Catherine was comfortable doing things in the way she knew how.

As people discovered Catherine was available for speaking engagements, she was invited to women's missionary meetings and pastors' wives retreats. She was popular as a banquet speaker, too. Sometimes she traveled with Everett in his church visitation.

Then, people began saying, "Everett should be president of Malone College."

"Oh, my!" said Catherine. "We're used to working in the villages of India. How can we work with college people? I have a hard time feeling like this could be God's plan."

Catherine and Everett prayed about it and talked about it. They finally decided, "We will agree to Everett being president of Malone College if *everyone* at the board meeting next week is 100 percent sure."

To each other they said, "That will likely never happen."

The next week they received the message, "We are all 100 percent sure."

*   *   *

The Cattells moved to Canton, Ohio, where Everett was installed as the college president.

Catherine found it hard to adjust. "Everett, I just don't belong here," she said. "Everything matters—hats, gloves, just everything! I don't know about such things. In China and India we had more important things to think about."

Catherine did not have an appropriate hat. Two kind women said, "We'll buy a hat for you." The lovely silver fur hat lasted Catherine for the rest of her life.

She also faced the problem of correctly furnishing the president's home. Women offered assistance for that, too.

Catherine was always a gracious hostess. She served dinners to large groups who gathered in the Cattell home. All visitors received a hot cup of tea from Catherine. Everyone was important to her, no matter who they were. People of Malone College knew they could count on Catherine's prayers. She took an interest in their lives and often went out of her way to send an encouraging card or a special gift.

*   *   *

"Could we pray together?" asked a doctor's wife one day. "You can do a little Bible study with me, too." Catherine was happy for this opportunity. Soon she was leading a whole group of ladies in weekly Bible study.

About that same time she wrote a book for children to help them learn about India. She gave it the title, *The Flying Carpet*.

More and more people asked Catherine to lead women's Bible studies. She was happy giving spiritual counsel to the women. Even so, she longed for the villages of India. There were times she wished she could sit out under the gorgeous trees with her beloved Indian women.

Then she and Everett went back to visit India again.

While they were there, Catherine met a village woman one day who introduced her husband, their four sons, and one daughter. "I told you I would. And we are *all* Christians."

At first Catherine did not know what she meant. Then she remembered. "Once upon a time you were a little girl who collected the offering at our meeting under the trees. You promised that one day you would be a Christian and so would your family." Catherine beamed at the seven people standing before her. "I've prayed that you would be able to keep your promise."

On another occasion Catherine attended a retreat with Indians from many parts of India and Nepal. Anna Nixon, another missionary, introduced her to a woman from Assam, located in the mountains of North India. "She's the woman, Catherine, who walks all over the mountains of Assam using the Bible lessons from your book *That They May Know.*"

Catherine clasped the Indian woman's hand. Then she thought, "Yes, my book of lessons *is* going where I could never go. Thank You, Lord!"

* * *

The next year Catherine wrote a family history. She had no notion of publishing it, but Everett suggested the idea. Others thought it would be worthwhile, too. She called it *From Bamboo to Mango.*

"We like this book about your life," many people told her.

The year after that she and Everett went back to Taiwan. They visited Barbara and her husband, John Brantingham, and their children, Jeanne, David, Jonathan, and Tim, who were missionaries there.

Catherine felt right at home in Taiwan. The Chinese language came back to her mind easily. Barbara arranged for her to lead Bible studies for several different groups of women.

Everett spent time teaching students at a seminary on the island. Even though he was often sick, it turned out to be a good year for Catherine.

Back in the United States, Catherine was constantly invited to speak and write. She wrote a column called "Over the Teacup" for the *Evangelical Friend* magazine. Years later, these articles were published as a book.

She and Everett moved to Columbus, Ohio. One day a woman called on the phone and asked Catherine to lead a Bible study group in her community. Several ladies came to the first meeting. Some already believed in God. Some did not. This group continued to meet with Catherine as their leader. Sometimes she wished that instead of sitting in their large, fancy homes she could be back out under the mango trees. "I would feel more natural in the pleasant Indian shade, wearing my comfortable sari," she thought.

"Please help me, God," Catherine prayed. "These women are asking questions no one has ever asked me before." God answered her prayer and helped her know how to talk to these wealthy women in ways they could understand.

Soon the Cattells made plans to move to Friendsview Manor in Newberg, Oregon. Before they completed all of the arrangements, Catherine met with another great sorrow.

Everett became ill and died.

Once again God helped Catherine through hard days. In a few months she said goodby to Mary and her husband, Fred Boots, and left for Oregon. There she began the task of putting things in order in room 216 at the retirement home.

She arranged thin, dainty china cups on the shelf. They helped Catherine recall occasions when she had visited in an Indian palace. That time someone had poured tea from a shining silver teapot. She remembered tea served in simple homes of the villagers, too. This tea was stirred by the hostess' finger before she poured it from brass or earthenware jugs.

Catherine placed her handsomely carved wooden table beside the chair. She hung her delicate Chinese fan and oriental pictures on the wall. All of these were reminders of India and China. The lands and their people would forever be a part of her.

All the time she was settling in, she prayed, "Lord, what will I do here? I don't know if I'll belong. I'm available, though, if anyone wants to come to talk or pray." She kept in regular contact with her family that after a while included two more grandsons, Stan and David Boots, and a great granddaughter named Leigh Owens.

Women of the church and community became acquainted with Catherine. Some of them came to her room to talk and pray. She was always interested in them and never failed to practice her Sunnyslope hospitality. Her guests were cheered by cups of good, steaming hot tea, served with cookies or crackers.

Catherine had many invitations to speak in places near Newberg and in places far away. Then another invitation arrived one day. It was for something she had never dreamed of doing!

Mango

Chapter 10

ANGELS LED THE WAY

Catherine blinked twice, just to be sure she was seeing the words correctly.

"Dear Grandmother. I will be going to China soon in connection with my job. I want you to go with me. We will find all of the places you remember from your childhood."

Catherine stared at this letter from her granddaughter, Jeanne Owens. She had never imagined she would have an opportunity to go back to China.

"A visit from a former missionary might cause trouble for the Chinese Christians", she thought. "Life is difficult for them. I wouldn't want to make things worse."

Before Catherine knew whether she should go or not, the doctor ordered major surgery for her. "Going to China is surely out of the question now," she said.

However, as she recovered, people she trusted encouraged her. "You should go," they said.

Catherine still felt unsettled about it. "Lord, give me a sign that *You* want me to go. Give me a date and this will help me have a definite idea."

Before noon that same day she opened a letter postmarked Taiwan. It said, "Please come to be the speaker for our missionary women's retreat here on the island." The next sentence told the exact days they wanted her to be there.

"Thank You, God," Catherine said joyfully. "This is my sign. I will go there first, then to China with Jeanne."

*   *   *

"This is China and I love it!" Catherine declared as they rode through the city of Shanghai in a taxi. She could hardly wait for Jeanne to finish her work so they could go on to Nanking.

At last they climbed aboard the rickety Chinese train. "It's exactly as I remember it," Catherine said. "Same old train . . . same old look about it. And of course no tea available." People crowded in and sat everywhere, just as they had done for so many years.

They hired a taxi in Nanking. "We're going to find the Quakerage," Jeanne promised.

The Friends Church Catherine remembered so well was gone. In its place was an enormous hotel. "Perhaps it will be harder to find the Quakerage than I thought, Jeanne. But we will find it. God gave me a promise this morning. He said, 'I will give you an angel to show you the way.' "

There was no sign of the Quakerage anywhere. Nothing looked familiar to Catherine. "This is dangerous for two American women to be snooping around alone," she whispered, taking hold of Jeanne's arm.

In the next breath, she said, "This hotel is on the ground where the Friends church once stood. And we know the Quakerage was directly across the street. It just has to be here."

Tall buildings crowded close together along the streets with new names Catherine did not recognize. Little alleys wound in and out between the buildings. The two women walked and walked. Finally Catherine spoke to a gateman.

"I was born in China and we are looking for the Quakerage."

The man's face crinkled into a smile. "I'm a Quaker. I'll take you there." He hurriedly led the way into a little alley.

And then Catherine saw what she was looking for. There was the Quakerage, surrounded on all four sides by immense high-rise buildings.

The Quakerage of Catherine's childhood had been the center of a carefully tended yard. Now all of that rolling green grass was gone. So was the great camphor tree. The bamboo was missing, also. All around the house was a cluster of run-down shacks. "It looks like the slums," Catherine thought sorrowfully.

The gateman led the way inside. "A family lives in each room," he explained. Catherine entered the parlor. Directly across was the circular stairway leading upstairs. "I used to slide down the banister when no one who would tell on me was looking," she laughingly told the others.

Upstairs, Catherine groaned when she saw a puddle that stretched the whole length of the hall. These days no one cared enough to mend the leaky roof. A big pile of dirt and garbage blocked her way to the room where the little girl Catherine went so fearfully each night.

She turned and slowly went back down the stairs. "You were the angel the Lord promised me today," Catherine told the gateman.

On Sunday they struck out for Luho. Catherine was sure she could find the Friends church. However, it turned out to be different there, too. Catherine looked about in dismay. "The city wall isn't here. And the gate is gone. I don't know where the church is after all."

"Listen," said Jeanne. "Someone is singing hymns." They followed the sound and ended up right in front of the Luho Friends Church.

The service was already well underway. Catherine and Jeanne crept in quietly. "We mustn't cause trouble," Catherine whispered. All 600 Chinese quickly became restless at the sight of the two foreigners.

"Do something quick, Lord," Catherine prayed.

An older Chinese woman rose from her place in front and walked toward the back of the church, quieting the people. Catherine leaned over the

Silk-Cotton in flower

Mohwa

Banyan

end of the bench and whispered in Chinese, "I'm Charles DeVol's little sister."

A smile broke out on the Chinese woman's face. She nodded knowingly, then sat down by Catherine and patted her arm. Others in the congregation calmed and the service continued.

Catherine enjoyed every minute of the worship hour. "It's just like it used to be," she thought contentedly. Afterward, the pastor took them to see how Peace Hospital looked now. Then he walked with them to the house where the DeVols had lived so long before. "You should know this is now the Communist headquarters," he explained. All the time they were walking through the house, Jeanne was busy taking pictures. Then it was time to say thank you and goodbye to the pastor.

"You, too, have been an angel of the Lord sent to lead us," Catherine told him gratefully.

* * *

Back home in Oregon, Catherine continued in her gracious manner, generous with her hospitality. Her strength gradually declined, but even so she remained interested in China and India. On July 3, 1986, Catherine died.

Her family and many friends gathered in two memorial services, one in Oregon and the other in Ohio. God comforted them as they thought about Catherine, her happiness under the Indian trees, and how she obeyed God no matter what. Everyone felt glad they would someday see her again in Heaven.